OWJC
3/13

ACCOLADES FOR THE ALDO ZELNICK COMIC NOVEL SERIES

An alphabetical adventure for middle-grade readers 7 to 13

2009 Book of the Year Award, juvenile fiction, *ForeWord Reviews*

2010 Colorado Book Award, juvenile literature

2010 Mountains & Plains Independent Booksellers Association Regional Book Award

2010 *Creative Child* magazine Seal of Excellence

Winter 2010 Kids' Next Indiebound selection

2011 CYBIL nomination

2011 Independent Publisher Silver "IPPY" Award

2011 *Creative Child* magazine Preferred Choice Award

2011 Quid Novi Award, first prize

2011 Moonbeam Children's Book Award, silver medal for comic/graphic novel

2011 Top 10 Educational Children's Products - Dr. Toy

2012 Book of the Year Award, kids' fiction, *Creative Child* magazine

WHAT READERS ARE SAYING:
(kid comments are in Aldo's handwriting)

"It was the funniest book I have ever read.
The illustrations are hilarious. It is better than
Diary of a Wimpy Kid."
— Tavis

"The Aldo Zelnick books keep getting better and better."
— Mary Lee Hahn, teacher and readingyear.blogspot.com blogger

"You will laugh out loud—I guarantee it. The books are THAT funny."
— Becky Bilby, inthepages.blogspot.com

"I've been waiting for a series to come along that could knock Wimpy Kid off its pedastel as the most popular series in my library. Well, this may be it: the Aldo Zelnick Comic Novels. Save room on your shelves for 26 volumes!"
— Donna Dannenmiller, elementary librarian

"Aldo is pretty awesome in my book."
— Dr. Sharon Pajka, English professor, Gallaudet University

"The other night I caught my 8-year-old twins giggling on the living room couch as they took turns reading *Artsy-Fartsy* aloud to each other. Then one morning I found it on their nightstand with a headlamp resting on the cover from the previous night's under-cover reading. That's a true badge of honor in this house. You hit this one out of the park."
— Becky Jensen

Glitch

AN ALDO ZELNICK COMIC NOVEL

Written by Karla Oceanak

Illustrated by Kendra Spanjer

BAILIWICK PRESS

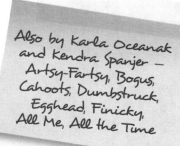

Also by Karla Oceanak
and Kendra Spanjer —
Artsy-Fartsy, Bogus,
Cahoots, Dumbstruck,
Egghead, Finicky,
All Me, All the Time

Published by:
Bailiwick Press
309 East Mulberry Street
Fort Collins, Colorado 80524
(970) 672-4878
Fax: (970) 672-4731
www.bailiwickpress.com
www.aldozelnick.com

Manufactured by:
Friesens Corporation, Altona, Canada
October 2012
Job # 79523

Book design by:
Launie Parry
Red Letter Creative
www.red-letter-creative.com

ISBN 978-1-934649-25-1

Library of Congress Control Number: 2012918667

21 20 19 18 17 16 15 14 13 12   7 6 5 4 3 2 1

Dear Aldo —
Happy first gift
of Christmas,
my little gherkin.* 
Here's hoping for a
December to remember.
♡ Goosy ♡

ALDO,

Glad tidings. I have
been given to understand
that you are a "G.*" Ha-ha.
(I am a modern slang
aficionado, you know.)

— Mr. Mot

WHO'S WHO

ME - ALDO ZELNICK.

GRISWOLD, OUR GOSSIPY* GNOME* IN THE HOME.

MY BEST FRIEND, JACK.

MY OTHER FRIENDS, BEE (WHO CELEBRATES CHRISTMAS), AND TOMMY GELLER (WHO CELEBRATES HANUKKAH), AND DANNY (CHRISTMAS).

SOME RANDOM GERBIL* WHO FINAGLED HIS WAY INTO THIS STORY.

MR. MOT, NEIGHBOR, WORD GUY, AND PICTURE TAKER.

MY GRANDMA, GOOSY. GLASS-BLOWER AND HOLIDAY DECORATOR.

SANTA (JUST COVERING MY BASES).

BACON BOY, STAR OF MY VERY OWN COMICS.

MY FAMILY. MOM, DAD, MY BROTHER, TIMOTHY, AND OUR DOG, MAX.

BEE'S FAMILY OF TREE HUNTERS, THE GOODES. MR. GOODE, MRS. GOODE, AND VIVI.

MR. KRUG, MY 5TH GRADE TEACHER, AND MR. FODDER, MY CAFETERIA GUY.

9

CHRISTMAS COUNTDOWN

Guess what my mom just handed me?! No, not the usual Saturday afternoon pile of clean laundry. It's my chocolate Christmas calendar!

EVERY DAY UNTIL CHRISTMAS, YOU GET TO OPEN A LITTLE PAPER DOOR WITH A NUMBER ON IT. BEHIND EACH DOOR IS AN ITTY-BITTY PIECE OF CHOCOLATE IN A DIFFERENT SHAPE. IT'S A CALENDAR AND A GERBIL*-SIZED DAILY SNACK, ALL IN ONE.

Yesss. That means today's December 1st... and <u>that</u> means just 24 more days till P to the R to the E to the S to the E to the N to the T to the S! PRESENTS!

Mom also said it's time for me to start making my list! Every year my brother Timothy and I write lists of the Christmas presents we're hoping for, and we tack them on the kitchen bulletin board.

Then *bam!*, a bunch of the things appear gift-wrapped and gorgeous* under the tree on Christmas morning. All in all, not a bad system.

And...now Mom's yelling up the stairs to me, saying I need to go bring in the mail from our mailbox at the end of the driveway. Sheesh. Can't a kid have a little yuletide planning time? BRB.

OK, somebody has been holding out on me all these years. How come I never knew about this fancy Christmas catalog? It came in today's

CHRISTMAS

THE GUMBALL PINBALL MACHINE

mail, and it's got the most fantastic toys and gizmos* I have <u>ever</u> <u>seen.</u> I mean, I would've put <u>lots</u> of this stuff on my Christmas lists before—if I'd only known it existed!

Take the **Inflatable Backyard Log Flume**, for example. Who doesn't want one of these?

Or the **All-Terrain Electric Transporter!** It's like an uber scooter you don't have to scoot yourself!

Or holy brain-freeze...

the **Classic Snow-Cone Cart!**

Welp, this magical catalog has opened up a whole new world of possibilities for my Christmas list. I mean, I don't wanna be a greedy* McSneedy, but apparently <u>somebody's</u> getting all this groovy* stuff. So why not me?

OH BROTHER, WHY ART THOU?

Whatever you do, don't have an older brother.

Maybe an older sister's OK...I'll never know, 'cuz God only seems to make boy Zelnicks...but an older brother is basically a torture device that smells like Gillette Power Rush deodorant.

Today was Timothy's 15th birthday, so he was all, "This is _my_ day, bro" and "We're totes having granola* and Greek yogurt* for breakfast." (He just made the junior varsity basketball team, but he acts like he's training for the Olympics.)

My family's tradition is that when it's your birthday (and you're a kid), you get to pick a family activity followed by dinner at a restaurant you choose. For his activity, Timothy decided on bowling, which seems easy until you try to hold a ball that weighs as much as a gallon of milk with 3 fingers and roll it down a skinny strip of wood. Oh, and if you don't throw it straight, your ball ends up in one of the twin Grand Canyons* on either side of the wood plank. So yeah, I got a lot of gutter balls. And a score not that much higher than Timothy's new age.

COULD THIS BE A NEW LEAGUE RECORD?!

COULD THIS EVEN BE CONSIDERED "BOWLING"?!

GUTTERS, AKA GRAND CANYONS

After gyros* at this restaurant called Garbanzo* (not bad, not bad), we came home for cake and ice cream, and Timothy opened his birthday presents. Being 15 means he can start learning to drive a car now, so he got a bunch of automotive gadgets,* like a steering-wheel cover for our old minivan and some new jumping cables, whatever those are.

I gave him a keychain that's a Gumby* action figure but also a flashlight. Plus he got some clothes and books and other stuff. And our grandma, Goosy, made him a cool coin dish out of glass.

LIKE A JUMP ROPE, ONLY BETTER!

NOT EVEN CLOSE. DON'T YOU KNOW ANYTHING ABOUT CARS?

Then it was time for him to open his "special" present. That's also a Zelnick family tradition. For your birthday and Christmas, you usually get a present that's bigger or specialer than all the little stuff. It's like the real movie after the previews.

So Dad brought out a giant box, which Timothy unwrapped. The present was one of those trick deals, where inside the giant box was a smaller wrapped box, and so on and so on until Timothy finally lifted out a tiny white box. And inside the tiny white box lay... an iPhone.

"No way!" I said.

"Way!" said Timothy. "Thanks!"

"You're in high school and you'll be driving soon, and since we're not with you all the time anymore," said Mom with a little gulp* in her voice, "we thought a smartphone would help you be more independent...and safer."

"They don't give those things away, so take good care of it, champ," said Dad.

"I will, Dad. Hey Aldo, I'll send you a text on my new iPhone!" Timothy grinned. "Oh wait. That's right...You don't have a cell phone."

Sheesh. Timothy got an awful lot of great presents today. Sure, I'll get stuff for my birthday in February too, but it seems like he scored gobs* of gifts! And Christmas is just around the corner, so he'll be getting even _more_! How is that fair?!

I _did_ get a present from Goosy today. Ever since I was little, she's given me something on Timothy's birthday too—a gift to distract me so I don't cry when it's time for Timothy to open his gifts. (When I was like 2! I wouldn't cry now. Probably.) Anyway, getting a present on Timothy's birthday is usually a good thing, but this time, not so much.

HAPPY SECOND GIFT OF CHRISTMAS, ALDO!

DANG. I WAS HOPING IT WAS A BOXFUL OF OF VIDEO GAMES.

Ack. I'm accidentally-on-purpose sticking the sweater down behind my dresser, where, with any luck, it will stay "lost" for a really, really long time.

HANUKKAH!
WHO KNEW?

I had to stay after school today to help Mr. Fodder in the cafeteria for a while (ahem...see *Finicky* for all the gory* details), so by the time I started to walk home, it was already getting dark. Since my best friend, Jack, wasn't with me like he usually is, I kept going straight instead of turning left at Jack's street and ended up by Tommy Geller's.

Tommy's a year older than me and Jack. He's in middle school now. He used to be a bully, but lately he got nice. I guess people <u>can</u> change. Anyway, as I was ambling down the sidewalk, I saw him standing inside his house, looking at me through the window. Here was the weird part: A couple lit candles were in front of him, and it was hard to see, but in the candlelight it looked like he was wearing a <u>bowl</u> on top of his head!

I stopped and waved. Tommy waved back, then a second later stuck his bowl-covered head outside his front door.

"Hey Aldo! Happy (hamumble)!" he said.

"Uh...Happy whatever you said to you!"

"Do you want to see our man Nora?"

"Is he your cat or something?"

Inside Tommy's house I found his brother and dad wearing the same bowls on <u>their</u> heads, only they weren't bowls, they were hats! And the whole family was standing next to this fancy candle-holder thingie that they use to light candles every night for the 8 nights of *Hanukkah* (not hamumble).

I stayed while the Gellers sang this weird non-English song to the candles, then as I turned to slip out, Mrs. Geller said, "Come have dinner with us tomorrow night if you'd like, Aldo. We're having *latkes*—fried potato pancakes."

I FOUND OUT IT'S CALLED A MENORAH (NOT OUR MAN NORA). TOMMY SHOULD REALLY SPEAK MORE CLEARLY.

Fried pancakes made out of <u>potatoes</u>! Maybe the Gellers will adopt me.

A WONDERFUL,
AWFUL IDEA!

I showed Jack the magical catalog after school today. We were sitting in the closet in my bedroom, which is also our winter fort, eating gingerbread cookies my dad just made.

"This Junior Secret Agent Spy Kit is *chido*," he said as he bit off his gingerbread man's head. (*Chido* means "cool" in Spanish, which is the other language Jack speaks.)

"Hey! You're eating something brown!"
I noticed. "Lemme see the catalog. Yeah, but that
spy kit is nothing. Check out this 9½-foot Remote
Controlled Bald Eagle!"

"Whoa. It costs $500."

"Ha. That's peanuts. Like, the World's
Largest Scrabble Game is $12,000! This catalog
has made me realize there are so many things
out there to want! Which reminds me. Hand me
that pad of paper, wouldja? I need to make my
Christmas list."

Paper in hand, I chewed on my pencil for a
few minutes as I daydreamed about all the present
possibilities. According to family tradition, I would
get one "special" gift. If I put more than
one big thing on my list, I'd risk not
getting what I wanted
most. But I wasn't
sure <u>which</u> big thing I
wanted most.

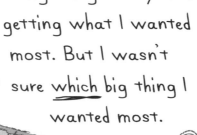

"This list-making businesses is tricky," I said finally. "It requires strategy. First, there's total gift count to consider. Timothy got a million cool little presents for his birthday on Sunday. That's pretty great. But then there's also the 'special' gift to consider. If I ask for something <u>too</u> big, I won't get it, or if I do, I probably won't get much other stuff. And the minute I turn in my list, it's all over. I've gotta nail it the first time."

Jack shrugged. "I just want a goethite geode* from the rock shop."

"Really? You don't want an Advanced Acrobatic Robot? Says here it can do backflips and play air-guitar solos! Plus, <u>you</u> get to have 2 Christmases—one at your Mom-house and one at your Dad-house! You're lucky...You can get whatever you want!"

WORLD'S LARGEST AIR GUITAR COLLECTION SOLD SEPARATELY.

"Nah. That catalog stuff is *loco* expensive."

I considered for a couple seconds before tiptoeing into what I said next, because it's touchy territory for 10-year-olds like me and Jack. "But you know who <u>doesn't</u> pay attention to price tags?" I suggested carefully. "The big guy with the white beard and the reindeer. So...we could always keep <u>that</u> option open." There. I'd said aloud what every red-blooded kid thinks at one time or another. I kept writing on the pad of paper, but I swiveled my eyeballs to look at Jack, to see how he'd react to the Santa card.

"True," he nodded thoughtfully. "I'm gonna make a list too. It can't hurt, anyway. Gimme a piece of that paper."

I'M AN EXPERT ON LISTS, AND THIS ONE IS GIGANTIC.

"Now you're talkin'!" And we wrote and wrote and wrote. When my pencil finally stopped, I had the longest Christmas list of my life. It was thrilling! But also...too much.

"I can't give this to Mom," I sighed. "She'll freak out."

"Just give her part of it," said Jack. "Tear off the top."

So I did. But I was still staring longingly at all the incredible stuff on the rest of the list when I had an idea. A wonderful, awful idea.

"What if I sent parts of the list to my relatives?" I said. "Like, I could cut it up into pieces and mail them to my Minnesota grandparents, and my aunt and uncle who live on the farm, and my Uncle Vinnie in Pennsylvania, etcetera...and I could end up with gifts galore!* Glorious* Gifts Galore—that's what I'll call the plan. Triple G!!" And I reached for the scissors.

"Hm," said Jack as I cut. "Sounds kinda complicated."

But I was too busy running to get my mom's address book and writing little notes and addressing envelopes and stickering stamps to ask him what he meant by that. When I was done letter-making and it was time for Jack to go home, I had a tidy little stack of Christmas cheer all ready for the mailman.

DID YOU HEAR THE JOKE ABOUT THE UNSTAMPED LETTER?

YOU WOULDN'T GET IT.

About then Mrs. Geller called my dad to tell him I really <u>was</u> invited to their house for Jewish dinner, and my dad told her that my great-grandfather was Jewish! Huh. No wonder I like Hanukkah-ing it up with Tommy so much. Tonight the Gellers gave me a bowl-hat of my own, and there were more lit candles and weird singing and afterward, crispy potato cakes with applesauce and sour cream. Yumbo! And then, <u>presents</u>.

TURNS OUT JEWISH KIDS GET HOLIDAY PRESENTS EVERY NIGHT FOR 8 NIGHTS!

Good thing I got in on this Hanukkah deal, because the Gellers gave me a spinning top with bizarre shapes on it called a "dreidel." Kinda weird, but I'm counting it toward my Triple G gift count anyway. And I was so enthusiastic about my family's long-lost Jewishness that the Gellers invited me back for more Hanukkah this week! Yesss.

Oh, and on my way to the Geller's house, I slipped all my Christmas list letters into the giant mailbox by the convenience store. So as I write this, they're probably already on their way to make this the best Christmas <u>ever</u>.

GNOME
IN THE HOME

I handed Mom my official Christmas list before school this morning.

"Here ya go," I said, grabbing a granola bar on my way out the door.

"Wait a second," she said. "It's torn. Where's the rest of it?"

Luckily I'd anticipated her question, so an answer was already warmed up and ready on my tongue. "I was just saving paper, Mom. Geez. Why waste a whole piece when you only need part of one?"

She frowned and gave me her Gorgon*- like Mom-gaze,* straight in the eyeballs. But I just smiled sweetly back, so she kissed me on the forehead, and off I went.

After school, Dad and Timothy were outside hanging Christmas lights. I set down my backpack and helped Dad untangle a strand while my athletic brother climbed up the ladder.

"I saw your Christmas list," Dad said to me. "Not too much on it really."

"Nah...Keepin' it real."

"Nothing special you want this year?"

Oops, I thought. I didn't include something biggish on the part of the list I'd given Mom? A definite glitch.*

"Um...," I said, improvising. "I did see this really cool snow-cone cart in a catalog."

"Sounds pretty extravagant."

"Yeah, that's why I didn't list it." (At least the part of the list I gave _you_ guys, I thought.) I fished around in my brain for another idea. "Well, I _do_ really want one of those video-gaming chairs with built-in speakers. But I know Mom won't go for that, so I didn't want to tell it to _her_."

"Hm," he said. "Something to think about, I guess."

Sweet! I'd managed to finagle a secret, extra gift request from Dad! So Triple G seemed to be getting off to a great start when, after dinner, Mom dragged out a bin of indoor Christmas decorations from our storage closet. "Here, Aldo, why don't you unpack a few things before you start your homework?"

Always helpful, I lifted the lid off the bin and *Gah!* There lay Griswold, gawking* up at me.

I'd forgotten all about Griswold! He's our Gnome* in the Home—another Zelnick family Christmas tradition. He's supposed to keep an eye on me and Timothy and report back to Santa— you know, about whether we've been naughty or nice.

I grabbed Griz from the bin. "Mom, Timothy and I are <u>way</u> too old for this."

"Awww...but you boys love Griswold!" she exclaimed, rushing over to rescue him. "Christmas wouldn't be the same without Griz! Besides, I've noticed that very young children aren't the <u>only</u> ones who need encouragement to behave well. (Meaningful pause.) Where should we put him this year? How about here, on the fireplace."

I glanced at Griswold and his permanent wide-eyed stare. I hadn't done anything wrong, had I? I'd just given people a few Christmas gift ideas, that's all. So why did I feel a little ping in my ribcage area? Must be indigestion from those enchiladas we had for dinner.

THE GIVER

I woke up early this morning, before anyone else, and shuffled downstairs to my advent calendar. From across the room, the foam gnome watched me punch open paper door number 6 and pry out the infinitesimal morsel of chocolate.

"What?" I asked him. "Didn't your mom teach you it's not polite to stare?"

Then the Christmas lists posted on the kitchen bulletin board caught my eye, and I padded over to inspect them.

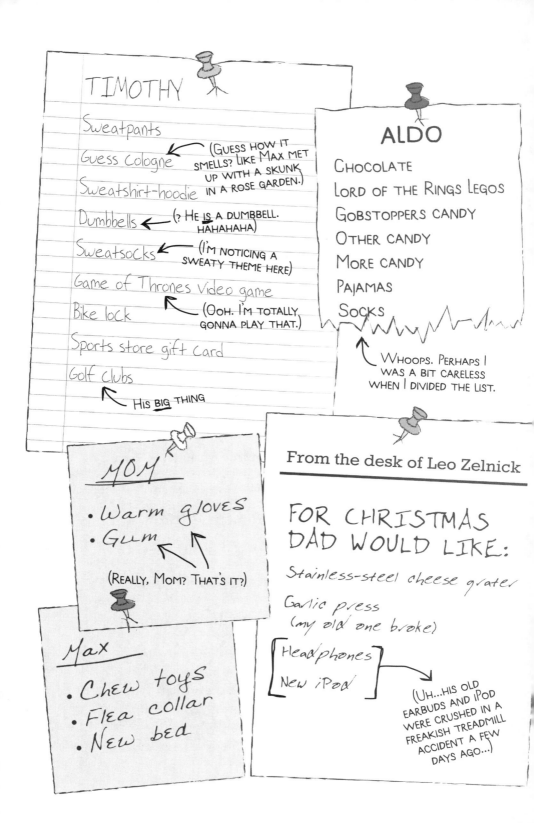

"Welp, it's time to start thinking about what I'm <u>giving</u> this year!" I said out loud. My voice echoed in the still-quiet morning kitchen. I glanced back at Griswold. "Yup, good thing I know what everyone wants now, so I can shop for <u>them</u>! That's what Christmas is all about, you know!"

Having put on a convincing show for Mr. Pointy Head, I went back upstairs to my room to get ready for school. That's where I am now, writing this. Hm. I guess I do need to start my Christmas shopping. Better see what my budget is...

OK, I just counted my money: $27 and 59 cents. I get 2 more allowances before Christmas... and maybe I can scrounge up a little couch money... so if I get presents for Mom, Dad, Timothy, and my grandma, Goosy...I can spend about $10 each. That's <u>plenty</u>.

THINGS YOU CAN BY FOR $10:

GAMESTOP GIFT CARD

10 GATOR-ADES (ON SALE!)

A DISH OF GRAVEL (FREE, SO $10 EXTRA FOR SLUSHIES)

Mr. Krug got us going on geometry* today in math. I thought a triangle was a triangle, but it turns out there are a bunch of different kinds:

Equilateral triangle

Right triangle

Isosceles triangle

Scalene triangle

Circle

PHONING IT IN

7

When I got home from dinner at the Gellers' tonight, Mom was in the kitchen writing out Christmas cards.

"How's Hanukkah treating you?" she asked.

"Great! Beef brisket and jelly-filled doughnuts. Plus, Tommy gave me <u>these</u> for a present!" I showed her the little bag of chocolate coins wrapped in shiny gold tinfoil.

THE CHOCOLATE COINS ARE CALLED GELT. THEY TASTE BETTER THAN THEY SOUND.

"What did you bring for Tommy?"

"Um..." Dang. Didn't consider that. "I figured I'd give him a Christmas present closer to Christmas. You know, since that's <u>my</u> holiday."

"Good thinking. Say, I got an odd e-mail from Caroline today," Mom went on. "She asked if you do a lot of scootering in the mountains. That's all it said."

MOMS... YOU NEVER KNOW WHAT DARK UNDERSTANDING LURKS BENEATH THE SWEET, PRETTY SHELL...

I spun around to hang up my coat and hide my getting-red face. Aunt Caroline must have gotten my Christmas letter, and her piece of the list must have the All-Terrain Electric Transporter on it! Gah! I didn't think about her telling my mom! Another glitch!

"Well, I don't mountain scooter very often, I guess..."

"I've never seen you on a scooter, period."

Her voice sounded pretty regular, not mad or anything, so I turned back to her. She was still writing a Christmas card like nothing had happened. Whew. So Aunt Caroline didn't spill the entire bean pot after all.

"Nah...scootering is one of those activities where you need to balance and move at the same time. I'm not gifted* at those."

Mom glanced up at the bulletin board. "I noticed your Christmas list doesn't have anything big on it, Aldo. Isn't there something special you want this year?"

Wow. There was that question again. I'd already suggested a gaming chair to Dad... Maybe I could ask Mom for something else?

"Well, I <u>was</u> thinking I'd feel safer with an iPhone...you know, since I walk back and forth to school every day and stuff."

She looked at me and raised an eyebrow. Behind her, Griswold kept right on gaping* with his big, googly eyes.

"And sometimes I want to go on really long bike rides, but I'm afraid I might get too far away and have a flat tire...I mean, it doesn't have to be an iPhone...it could be a plain old cell phone."

"Hm. I'm not buying the bike rides part...but getting you a cell phone is not a terrible idea."

When she looked back down at the Christmas card she was writing, I winked at old Griz. He'd somehow moved to the kitchen counter. Who'd have thought Mom would be so gullible?!* Triple G is gonna be a piece of cake. I don't know why I didn't think of it <u>years</u> ago.

GUM DROPS

GNOCCHI

GRAHAM CRACKERS

BACON BOY IN GLORIOUS GIFTS GALORE

YES! ASK FOR EVERYTHING YOU EVER WANTED! YOU DESERVE IT!

REALLY?! I CAN HAVE IT ALL?

YOU'RE ONLY A KID ONCE, SPORT!

YOU CAN'T HAVE IT ALL. WHERE WOULD YOU PUT IT?

I WANT AN INFLATABLE BACKYARD LOG FLUME, AND AN ALL-TERRAIN ELECTRIC TRANSPORTER, AND A CLASSIC SNOW-CONE CART...

SOMEBODY'S BEEN READING HIS CHRISTMAS CATALOGS!

ME? WELL I'VE BEEN DROOLING OVER THE CANINE TREADMILL AND THAT DOGGIE BED THAT PREVENTS SEPARATION ANXIETY...

OH CHRISTMAS TREE

After disco class today with Goosy (yes, she's still making me go to dance lessons with her on Saturday mornings), we drove to Goosy's house. She said she had an artistic dilemma she wanted my opinion on.

"All right. But are you gonna want me to be honest with you?" Goosy may be a pro artist and everything, but that doesn't mean I like everything she makes.

"Don't I <u>always</u> want you to be honest?"

"I guess so."

Being honest means not answering with a lie when someone asks you a direct question, I thought as we bounced on the bench seat of Goosy's purple pick-up truck. *But what if no one asks you the right question?* Then we rounded the corner onto Goosy's street.

"OK, here's my opinion," I said as we pulled up to her house. "It's...gaudy.*"

GAUDÍ
GEHRY
GOOSY!

IS THERE
EVEN A HOUSE
UNDER ALL
THAT STUFF?

"Aldo, no. It's not my
Christmas decorations I need your help
with. I'm not even done with those, silly!
It's the piece I'm working on. Let's go inside." We
went into her house and upstairs to the art studio,
which is where she does all her painting and sculpting
and artsy-fartsy stuff. "I'm making a glass
sculpture for the Denver airport," she said as she
opened the studio door, "and it's driving me bonkers."

And there in the middle of the floor stood a giant, sparkling pine tree.

"Gadzooks!* You made a Christmas tree out of glass?!"

"They wanted a sculpture to represent our state to the people from all over the world who travel in and out of our airport, so I proposed a Colorado Blue Spruce."

"Hey...that's the kind of tree my summer fort is under!"

"You're right. And I'm happy with how my glass tree turned out, but something's missing...and I can't figure out what."

"Our fort tree has a raccoon..."

"No, I don't think it needs a raccoon."

"Well...it looks kinda lonely... I know! Presents! It's a Christmas tree, too, so you could put presents all around it!"

"Hmmm. I <u>could</u> make glass boxes with frilly glass bows, all in different colors... That <u>would</u> be beautiful at Christmas time. Audacious idea, Aldo!"

"Yup, I'm pretty much an idea geyser* lately."

Then on her super-big computer screen,
Goosy showed me a picture of the spot inside the
airport where the sculpture will go.

"I wish I had one," I found myself saying.

"You'd get tired of a glass tree that took up
your whole living room."

"No, not the tree. The <u>computer</u>. If I had
a nice computer all for myself, I could use it to
help me do my art, just like you do." There I went
again, suggesting another big gift! And Goosy
<u>loves</u> giving me presents that encourage
my artsy-fartsy side.

COMPUTER,
COMPUTER,
SO SHINY
AND BRIGHT,
TO MY TRIPLE
G PLAN I
NOW YOU
INVITE.

"A computer, huh? Would you really use it to make art?"

"Sure!" And play games and watch YouTube videos, I thought.

"Well, Christmas is coming very soon!"

When I first launched Triple G, I didn't realize that it would just keep growing and growing. It's unstoppable, like the Incredible Hulk. Or my occasional gaseousness,* once it escapes.

I'VE FOUND THAT CONTINUOUS GASEOUSNESS IS MORE SATISFYING THAN OCCASIONAL FLATULENCE.

REMEMBER JACK'S STINKY DOG, SLATE?

MALL HAUL

I asked Mom to take me shopping today so I could buy presents.

"For yourself or for other people?" she asked.

"For other people, of course!"

"Just checking."

So we went to the mall and walked all around. The place was crammed with shoppers carrying fistfuls of bags. The fa-la-la-la-la music jingling from the speakers had us all feeling festive.

At the sporting goods store, I showed Mom the golf clubs I thought Timothy would like, and I bought him a 6-pack of orange golf balls. I didn't see anything good for Goosy, but for Dad, the kitchen store had a few cheese graters to choose from. I picked the most expensive one, even though it blew my budget. When it comes to cheesy-food-making equipment, you've gotta go with the best.

"It makes me happy to see you think about other people," smiled Mom.

Right about then we walked by a Christmas tree covered with scraps of paper. "Oh look, it's the Giving Tree!" said Mom. On every piece of paper was written the name and age of a kid and 3 things that kid wants for Christmas.

"Where are the forms?" I asked, recognizing a Triple G opportunity when I saw it. "I need to fill one out."

"No, Aldo, these are kids whose families can't afford to buy extras like Christmas presents. Since you're in such a generous mood, let's choose 2 tags—one for you and one for Timothy. That way each of you can shop for a child less fortunate than you."

"I don't have enough money!"

"Your dad and I can provide the money. You just need to provide the thoughtfulness."

"Oh. I might be running out of that too." But even though I was getting tired of shopping, I picked a kid.

Name: Griffin
Age: 10
Wishes: Jeans, size 12
Twin bed sheets
Legos

So we stopped at the boring department store for Griffin's jeans and sheets. Geez, what kid loves bed coverings?

The toy store was gridlock,* but I managed to squeeze through to the lego aisle and grab Griffin my favorite Lord of the Rings set. I wonder if he'd mind if I preassembled a few parts for him before we wrap it up...

Then on our way out of the mall, we went past Gerald's—you know, that fancy jewelry store from the TV commercials, the one where the mom goes all gaga* because the dad gives her a bracelet? Puh-lease. Anyway, as we walked by their display window, Mom gasped.*

"What? Did you also just realize we forgot to have a Cinnabon?" I said.

"Come look at this garnet* ring. It's exactly like the one my Grandma Gracie used to wear."

I looked at the ring. It looked like a ring.

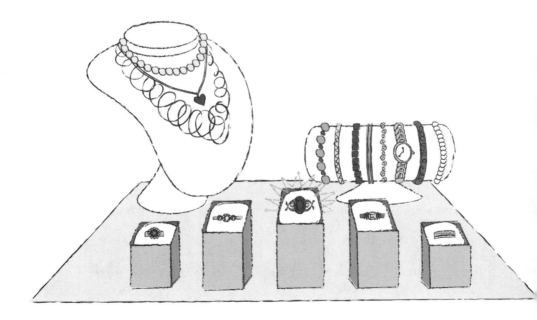

"OK, it's great and all, but my feet are flattening. Let's make like a bakery truck and haul our buns out of here."

When we got home, I told Dad (who was sitting by the crackly-warm fire below the mantel where Griswold perched) all about my day spent shopping for <u>other people</u>, including spending my own money and picking out gifts for needy children.

Then as I was loading the dishwasher after dinner, our neighbor friend Mr. Mot came over to take

our Zelnick family Christmas photo. I don't know how, but Mom found the new holiday sweater I'd "misplaced," and when she asked me to put it on, I didn't give her even one ounce of guff.*

For the record, today was 100% dedicated to thinking of others. Which is 100% exhausting, so I'm turning out my light now and going to visions-of-sugarplums land. To all a goodnight.

p.s. Uh-oh. Dad just poked his head into my room to say that Uncle Vinnie texted him this message: ———————>

"Do you have any idea what he's talking about?" asked Dad. *There it was...a direct question.*

"Oh, I just gave him a few gift ideas. When Christmas rolls around every year, he always says he doesn't know what to get me." And...*I gave an honest answer.*

"OK. Goodnight sport."

"Night, Dad."

Whew. I'm starting to get a glimmer* of what Jack meant by Triple G being complicated...

JOY TO THE WORLD

Tonight was our school holiday band concert.

Sheesh. They've even brainwashed <u>me</u> into saying that now! Ever since I started school, I was told not to say "Christmas concert" because not everyone celebrates Christmas, but where I live, pretty much everyone except Tommy Geller <u>does</u> celebrate Christmas, so the whole thing is completely absurd.

Anyway...when we were getting ready to go to the concert, Mom told me to put on that ~~ugly~~ new sweater Goosy gave me.

"Uhhh...no," I said.

"Don't be silly. It's <u>perfect</u> for a holiday concert. It even has bells!"

"Bells are for sleighs and reindeer. And maybe elves. Not even sure about elves."

"Goosy will be expecting you to wear it, Aldo."

YOU TRY DELIVERING PRESENTS ALL HUSH-HUSH IN THE MIDDLE OF THE NIGHT WHILE WEARING JINGLE BELLS. WHOSE GREAT IDEA WAS THAT, ANYWAY?

Gah. But since I didn't want to cool down the warm feelings Mom's been having for me lately, and because Goosy might be making a big Triple G contribution, I wore the sweater and gave them both a big smile and wave when I walked onto the stage.

What with the bright lights and the heavy sweater and the energetic B-L-O-W-I-N-G into my trumpet, it was getting pretty hot up there. We were just launching into our big finale, "Joy to the World," when I started feeling really groggy.* Next thing you know, I'm staring up at Jack's ginormous* face.

You fainted, amigo. On stage. During the concert. I thought I was gonna have to give you mouth-to-mouth.

Then my band teacher, Mrs. Dulcet, loomed into view. "Drink this," she said, hoisting me back into my chair and handing me a cup of water. "Don't play. Just sit."

The crowd clapped and whistled when they realized I wasn't dead after all. I waved again, two-thirds embarrassed but one-third enjoying the glory. As I sat and listened to the sounds of "Joy to the World" all around me, it occurred to me that tonight was probably good not only for a sympathy bump in my Christmas present count, but also ice cream on the way home. And when I'm right, I'm right.

DEAR SANTA

Tonight was the last night of Hanukkah, so the Gellers called and invited me for one final celebration.

"What did you think of our Festival of Lights, Aldo?" Mr. Geller asked as we sat down to dinner. We'd already finished the candles and singing part. He passed me a platter of strange, beige-colored meatloaf slices, each topped with a slice of carrot. "We've enjoyed sharing our holiday with you. This is gefilte fish,* by the way."

"Oh, OK." I reached up to straighten my bowl-hat. I don't think I could be Jewish because it constantly goes askew on my squiggly hair. "Well, it's cool that you know how to sing in a different language. Plus, you guys get presents for 8 nights!"

WHATEVER HAPPENED TO MILK AND COOKIES?

"They're not as big as Christmas presents," said Tommy.

"And we still have school over Hanukkah," groaned Tommy's older brother, Dagan.

"Well, Hanukkah isn't our biggest holiday, but Christmas is everywhere this time of year!" said Mrs. Geller. "Every faith has its own traditions."

After I'd thanked the Gellers and was walking home, I thought about faith and traditions. Usually I have complete faith that I'll get most of the Christmas presents I want...but this year, since Griswold is being extra nosy and Triple G has had some gaffes,* I was feeling not so sure.

That's when I decided to go straight to the Big Man himself. Yes, I, Aldo Zelnick, a 10-year-old 5th grader, wrote a letter to Santa.

The way I figure it, it's like a Christmas morning insurance policy or a letter to the editor of the gift universe. Here's what it said:

December 11

Dear Santa,

How are things up there at the North Pole? Any ice left these days? I know I haven't written in a few years, but I've been busy. Plus, I'm 10 now. So yeah.

I'm writing because I do have quite a few requests this year. After all, it's my 10th Christmas anniversary—which, if you think about it, is kind of a big deal. Anyway, I'd like Lord of the Rings Legos, a cell phone, movie DVDs, a computer, a video-gaming chair, an American Girl doll (kidding! just making sure you're actually reading this), a snow-cone cart (does it come in Slushie too? because if it does, then Slushie), Green Lantern pajamas, a backyard log flume, an electric scooter, a year's supply of Gobstoppers, and any new video games you happen to have extras of lying around. For my stocking, chocolate and gift cards.

⟶

(CONTINUED FROM PAGE 1)

Also, what's the deal with sending foam gnomes to spy on kids? Isn't trust the basis of every good relationship? Just in case our Gnome in the Home, Griswold, is giving you the wrong impression, I <u>have</u> been good this year and I'm not a greedy McSneedy. I'm just a regular kid trying to figure out how to win at the game of life. And, ya know: no guts, no glory!

With good cheer,

Aldo Zelnick

p.s. When you see a glass of chocolate milk and a bowl of gherkins,* you'll know you're in the right house because that's what I'll be leaving out for you. You're welcome!

THE GAME OF LIFE

THE TININESS OF THESE CHOCOLATES IS REALLY STARTING TO GET MY GOAT.*

Since I'm on a niceness kick, I shared some candy canes my mom gave me with Jack and Bee. We were playing The Game of Life board game in the fort after school today.

"I shopped for my family yesterday," I mentioned as I added twins to my little plastic station wagon. "And I bought presents for a poor kid. We got a couple of those Giving Tree tags at the mall."

"Nice!" said Bee. "We're giving a goat to a family in Africa."

"Um...I'm pretty sure the goat will eat the packing peanuts." I drew a Career card. "*Gah!* I don't want to be an Athlete!"

"We're not shipping a goat, silly. We're just paying for a goat that's already in Africa to be donated to a family that needs one."

"I bet goats aren't as good of pets as Maxie."

"It's not a pet, Aldo. Goats make milk. Duh."

"I gave my Christmas list to my mom," said Jack. "Ya know—the list I made here the other day?"

"Yeah? And?"

Jack paid the bank a pink $20,000 bill for his burst pipes. "And she said I was being a greedy McSneedy."

"Hey! That's _my_ phrase that I made up!"

Esto es demasiado muchos! (This is way too many!)

"She didn't use those words, but that's what she meant."

"Why? How many things are on your list?" asked Bee, moving her game piece backwards to get a second college degree.

"About 79," said Jack. "But 71 of them were kinds of rocks."

"I agree with your mom," said Bee. (Surprise, surprise.) "Kids like us who already have a lot should do more giving than getting at Christmas."

"I'm giving!" I protested. "And besides, writing down gift ideas is just being helpful. It's up to the gift-givers to decide what to actually buy. Plus, there are tons of kids who have way more than we do. Like...Grover!"

Grover's the boy in our class who has it all (besides a good name)—every gaming system, every game, a smart phone, his own laptop, the coolest sneakers, a suntan in the wintertime from vacations to far-away islands. I bet he even has a Classic Snow-Cone cart in his bathroom.

"So you're saying we're in the middle," said Bee as she whizzed her station wagon past mine. "We're not have-nots and we're not have-it-alls. I guess that's kind of true."

"All I know is I crossed 75 things off my list," said Jack, "even the goethite geode."

"Dang," I said. "Welp, I'm still going strong with Triple G. Hey! I wrote a bestseller! That'll be $80,000, please."

I WONDER IF ANY OF MY SKETCHBOOKS WILL EVER BE BESTSELLERS....

Of course, since I mentioned Triple G, Bee made me explain the plan to her. I admitted I hadn't really thought it all through and it's getting a little glitchy.

"Good!" said Bee as she retired to Millionaire Estates with her fat stack of Life cards. "I hope it gets glitchier."

After we'd finished The Game of Life, we opened the fort door for some fresh air...and guess who was standing there, on my bedroom floor!

"Awww, where'd this cute gnome come from?" asked Bee.

"Ahh! He's spying!" I said.

"That's Griswold," Jack explained to Bee. "He's supposed to keep an eye on Aldo for Santa." Jack remembers him from other Christmases. When we were little, Jack and I would stuff Griz into a kitchen cupboard or throw a kitchen towel over his head—and once we plunged him into a snowbank—so he couldn't watch what we were doing. But somehow he always found his way out again...

"Yay for Griswold," said Bee. "Because somebody needs to keep an eye on Mr. Greedy McSneedy."

MY 12 DAYS OF CHRISTMAS

A few minutes ago I opened door number 13 on my advent calendar...which means there are only 12 days left till Christmas! But sheesh, those chocolate bits are tiny. So even though Dad said dinner will be ready in an hour, my starvation alarm is about to go off. BRB.

OK, I went back down to the kitchen to grab a little grub,* but Mom shooed me away. *Gah!* She pulled out the old "you'll spoil your appetite" (which never happens) and sent me away snackless.

So I'm sitting here <u>famished</u>. Did you ever notice that when your stomach is empty, your brain fills up with thoughts of food, which just makes you hungrier? I can't stop thinking about food...

The 12 Days of Christmas: the Hungry Version

On the **first day** of Christmas,
    I'm gonna go get me...
a 44-ounce cherry-lime Slushie.

On the **second day** of Christmas, I'm gonna go get me...
2 turkey legs and a 44-ounce cherry-lime   Slushie.

On the **third day** of Christmas, I'm gonna go get me...
3 gravy boats, 2 turkey legs,
and a 44-ounce cherry-lime Slushie.

On the **fourth day** of Christmas, I'm gonna go get me...
4 fried cheese curds, 3 gravy boats, 2 turkey legs,
AND DIPPING SAUCE   and a 44-ounce cherry-lime Slushie.

On the **fifth** day of Christmas, I'm gonna go get me...
5 POUNDS OF BACON!...

4 fried cheese curds,
3 gravy boats,
2 turkey legs, and
a 44-ounce
cherry-lime Slushie.

On the **sixth** day of Christmas, I'm gonna go get me...
6 Cokes a'fizzin', **5 POUNDS OF BACON!...**

4 fried cheese curds,
3 gravy boats,
2 turkey legs, and
a 44-ounce
cherry-lime Slushie.

On the seventh day of Christmas, I'm gonna go get me...
   7 churros crunchin',
   6 Cokes a' fizzin',
5 POUNDS OF BACON!
4 fried cheese curds,
   3 gravy boats,
      2 turkey legs,
         and a 44-ounce cherry-lime Slushie.

On the eighth day of Christmas, I'm gonna go get me...

8 Twinkies twinklin',

7 churros crunchin', 6 Cokes a' fizzin', **5 POUNDS OF BACON!**
4 fried cheese curds, 3 gravy boats, 2 turkey legs,
and a 44-ounce cherry-lime Slushie.

On the ninth day of Christmas, I'm gonna go get me...
9 chickens frying,

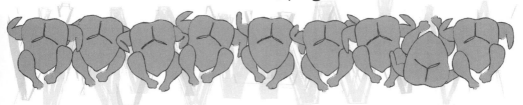

8 Twinkies twinklin', 7 churros crunchin', 6 Cokes a'fizzin',
5 POUNDS OF BACON! 4 fried cheese curds, 3 gravy boats,
2 turkey legs, and a 44-ounce cherry-lime Slushie.

On the tenth day of Christmas, I'm gonna go get me...
10 lobsters dripping, 9 chickens frying,
8 Twinkies twinklin', 7 churros crunchin', 6 Cokes a'fizzin',
5 POUNDS OF BACON! 4 fried cheese curds, 3 gravy boats,
2 turkey legs, and a 44-ounce cherry-lime Slushie.

On the eleventh day of Christmas, I'm gonna go get me...
11 pizzas piping, 10 lobsters dripping, 9 chickens frying,
8 Twinkies twinklin', 7 churros crunchin', 6 Cokes a'fizzin',
5 POUNDS OF BACON! 4 fried cheese curds, 3 gravy boats,
2 turkey legs, and a 44-ounce cherry-lime Slushie.

On the twelfth day of Christmas, I'm gonna go get me...

12 doughnuts dunking
11 pizzas piping
10 lobsters dripping
9 chickens frying
8 Twinkies twinklin'
7 churros crunchin'
6 Cokes a'fizzin'
5 POUNDS OF BACON!
4 fried cheese curds
3 gravy boats
2 turkey legs...
and a 44-ounce
cherry-lime Slushie.

TA-DA!

SUGAR AND SPICE AND ALDO'S SO NICE

14

You know how some guys like to fix up cars or build stuff? That's how my dad is with baked goods—an enthusiastic do-it-yourselfer.

YOU'RE MESSING WITH GENDER STEREOTYPES.* NOT SURE HOW I FEEL ABOUT THAT.

THAT'S HOW I ROLL!

Today was Christmas-cookie-making day at our house. I could tell the minute I walked in after school. On the kitchen island sat a gargantuan* bag of flour, the sugar bin, the big green mixer, baking trays, and everything else you need to make circles of deliciousness galore. Dad had already rolled up his sleeves and put on his favorite red apron.

"Cookie dough for dinner? Uh, yeah!!" I washed my hands, tied on my matching apron, and we got to work.

We started with cranberry-macadamia-white chocolate chunk. While Dad dumped butter and sugar into the mixer bowl, I measured flour using the scrape-off-the-mound-with-a-knife method he'd taught me when I was little.

"Do you need me to take you shopping to get a present for Mom?" Dad asked, cracking an egg with one hand.

"Did you look at her list? I don't know what to get her! Plus, I ran out of money already."

"She wants gum. You can probably scrounge up enough money for that, right?"

"I'm not getting her gum. That's dumb."

Dad spooned vanilla into the bowl, then it was time to add the nuts, cranberries, and white chocolate pieces. I poured them in and watched the mixer swirl them into a pretty red and gold and white pattern—a pattern that reminded me of...

"Hey, I know something Mom wants!" I remembered. "She went apoplectic over a ring at the mall."

"Your mom wants jewelry?"

"I know, right? She doesn't usually go for that girly stuff. But she said it's just like a ring her grandma had." I slipped my finger into the mixing bowl and scooped out my first bite of dinner.

"If I took you there later, could you show me which one?"

"Yup. Cuz I drew it in my sketchbook that day when we got home. Whenever I draw something, it gets locked into my brain."

Dad grinned. "You're a very useful child today."

I grinned back. "Who knew?"

"Still have your heart set on that video-gaming chair?"

Something about his question pushed my pause button for a second. Did I have my heart set on it? I played in a chair like that once—at Grover's house, at his birthday party—and it was one of the most memorable gaming experiences of my life. (Of course, Grover's gazillion*-inch flat-screen TV didn't hurt either.)

"They are pretty cool," I said. Griswold, back on the mantel, kept his googly eyes trained on me.

"Well it sounds like a good match then, 'cause you're pretty cool yourself."

After dinner, Dad drove me to the mall and I showed him the ring. He bought it and had it gift-wrapped. "It can be from both of us, sport," he said, patting me on the back.

Bee said I should concentrate more on giving than getting. But maybe it's like that karma thing Goosy taught me about a while ago: You get back what you give. Give a lot, get a lot. Only, I hope I don't get a garnet ring. That would be so dumb.

GOOD TREE HUNTING

You probably go to a store or a parking lot to buy a tame one, but every December we Zelnicks drive up into the mountains to cut down a wild Christmas tree. After all, here in Colorado, pine trees grow thicker than Mr. Mot's ear hair.

We always take Goosy's pick-up truck on tree day, so the tree has a bed to lie in on the way home. As we drive, we listen to an old recording of *The Grinch*—the one with the goofy* songs mixed in with the story. That's part of our tradition too, just like the thermos of hot chocolate and the sack of just-baked cookies for the celebration after we've cut the tree. Even though it involves some hiking, it's pretty much a great day. Usually.

YOU'RE A FOUL ONE, MR. GRINCH.
YOU'RE A NASTY, WASTY SKUNK.
YOUR HEART IS FULL OF UNWASHED SOCKS,
YOUR SOUL IS FULL OF GUNK,* MR. GRIII-INCH...

This year, Bee's family got invited to tag along. They followed behind us in their car. When we reached the tree-cutting forest, we all stepped out into the sparkly snow, squinched our eyes against the bright sun, and began to hunt.

I 'spose Christmas tree hunting is pretty much like any kind of hunting, except that foliage can't flee. But still, you have to walk around and check out a million trees to find the perfect one. That's because mountain evergreens aren't as isosceles trianglish as the ones on Christmas tree farms. Mom says the farm trees get haircuts as they grow so they'll turn out just the right shape and size for people's living rooms.

WE GOT THIS.

10 10

"Bet you 10 bucks I find a better tree than you," said Timothy as we set off. He's so competitive that he always tries to make everything into a contest.

"Tsk-tsk. Gambling is inappropriate during this blessed season," I said. But then I remembered Triple G and pictured a $10 bill on the very top of my present pile, like a crisp, green garnish.* "OK, you're on."

Timothy grinned and took off like Roadrunner.

"Help me find a tree!" I asked Bee. Actually, my voice might've sounded less askish and more orderish. "I need to beat Timothy!"

"All right! Don't get your long undies in a bunch."

So Bee and I zipped all around the snowy hill in search of a truly great Christmas tree. Every time we thought we'd spotted "the one," we'd get up close and find it was crooked or gangly* or missing branches on an entire side. All the while Bee gabbed* about the goat gift and how goats can live anywhere, even where it's dry and there's barely any grass, and how the family's children will have all the goat milk they want to drink plus some left over for making cheese. I put down my ear flaps.

"I think we're good on the goat info," I said after being told that families use goat poop to fertilize their gardens.

"OK. You pick a topic," groused* Bee.

"All right. My topic is: Silently Finding the Winning Tree."

Fortunately Bee got distracted just then. "Hey! This one's perfect!" she announced.

And sure enough, there in front of us stood the Christmas tree from heaven. We walked all the way around it for a 360-degree inspection. It was flawless.

"I found it!" I yelled as loudly as I could. "Mom! Dad! Timothy! Goosy!" Bee grimaced* and mumbled something that sounded like "Greedy McTreedy." I don't know what she's mad about. She doesn't deserve <u>all</u> the credit.

Timothy was the first to arrive at my perfect tree. "I found one too," he huffed. "Mom and Dad are over there falling in love with it right now."

So then we all had to galumph* back and forth, back and forth, comparing Timothy's tree to mine. They were both pretty awesome. Finally we took a family vote. Timothy and Mom picked Timothy's, and Dad and I picked mine. That left Goosy for the tiebreaker.

"Well I _am_ partial to pinecones," she said. "And Aldo's has some particularly gorgeous ones."

"Let's cut 'er down!" said Dad. I'd won!

89

We all took turns sawing except for Dad, whose sawing muscles are still healing from a basketball injury. The Goodes decided to take the tree Timothy had found, and soon they were sawing away too. We dragged the cut trees back to Goosy's truck and hoisted them in.

Then as the shadows got long, we shared our hot chocolate and cookies with the Goodes. The grown-ups gibber-gabbered,* and I heard Mom ask Bee's little sister, Vivi, what she wants Santa to bring her this year.

A GROOVY GIRLS DOLL NAMED GABRIELLE. AND A BABY GOAT!

Sheesh. The Goodes are obsessed with goats!

"What do <u>you</u> want for Christmas this year, Aldo?" asked Bee all sweet and innocent, like she wasn't popping open a giant can of worms.

"Um, I dunno...," I glowered* at her. "Welp, it's getting dark! Time to make like an evergreen tree and—"

"Aldo does want something special, don't you, Aldo," interrupted Mom. "And he's been so sweet lately, I think he just might deserve it!"

"So you told her after all?" said Dad to me.

"Well, I uh..."

"It is an expensive gift," said Goosy. "But I suppose it's something kids need today."

Oh no! This conversation had to stop. Immediately. I needed to create a distraction—and fast. Timothy was bent over, retying his boot laces. So, I jumped onto his back and clung like a monkey.

Timothy tipped me off to the side, which set me hurtling down the hill. Whew was all I could think as I rolled deeper and deeper into the darkening forest. My gloves were actually in my pockets, so once I stopped gyrating,* I figured, all I had to do was yell, "I found them!" then walk back up the hill. Surely the commotion I'd caused would have put an end to the Christmas gift gossip* by then.

But there in the shadows, I saw something.
Or should I say, someone. Just as I came to a stop
and lifted my snow-caked noggin from the ground,
I saw an isosceles triangle poking out from behind
one of the tree trunks.

And even though I was dizzy, I could swear I
glimpsed* two googly eyeballs beneath it. Griswold!

A chill not caused by the wintery coldness
made me shiver. I stood up and wiped the snow
from my face then looked behind the tree. Nothing.
But still, I'd seen what I'd seen.

If that darned gnome isn't staying in the
home anymore, Triple G may be in <u>serious danger</u>.

p.s. A warning in case you're thinking of hunting one: Wild Christmas trees always look way smaller out there in the forest than they actually are in real life. Guess we'll have to cut off the pineconey top of my prize-winner. *Sigh.*

And also, Griswold was in his usual spot on the fireplace mantel when we got home! When I picked him up and examined him for signs of forest gallivanting,* I found a single brown pine needle stuck to the bottom of his little foam boot. Hmmm...

GUSSYING UP* THE TREE

After Mom and Dad hung lights on the
Christmas tree today, they handed me and Timothy
our ornaments. Each of us has a shoeboxful of special
decorations—ones people have given to us or that we
picked out ourselves or made when we were little.

Like, the time my Grandma
Anderson took a trip to Africa, she
sent me this giraffe ornament. (It's
kind of fragile, so I accidentally
broke its neck right away. But
as you can see, I put it back
together, good as new.)

And I picked out this bacon-and-eggs ornament at the store myself when I was 3. The story goes that when we got home with the new ornament, Timothy, who was 6, broke off a piece of the bacon and told me to taste it. But instead I smelled it and sucked it up my nose. Mom had to yank it out with a tweezers.

IT BROKE HERE.

DON'T WORRY. IT'S GLUED BACK TOGETHER AND 100% BOOGER-FREE.

Lots of the items I lifted out of my box came attached with memories. As I carefully and lovingly hung my ornaments while Griswold looked on, Timothy sat on the couch and, one by one, launched his decorations at the tree.

"Stop throwing stuff!" I said. "You're spoiling my Christmas remembering."

"I'm hooking them, bro." Sure enough, most of the the ornaments he'd hurled were now bobbing from tree branches.

I tried to ignore him and kept placing my ornaments. But when I got to the paper gingerbread man I'd made in preschool, I decided it looked more like a grotesque* baby Gollum. I was just depositing it in the trashcan when Mom noticed.

"Don't throw it away! It's precious!"

"It's ruining my reputation as an artist."

"Oh don't be silly. The things you've made by hand are the things I cherish the very most!"

So I let Mom hang it on the tree, but when she wasn't looking, I moved it to the back branches, up against the wall, where nobody but the paint can see it.

Later, after dinner, I was in my room doing my Sunday night homework (I still don't get how that doesn't violate child labor laws) when Dad snuck in.

"So did you tell Mom about the gaming chair you want?" he whispered. "Before your tumble down the mountain yesterday, it sounded like she knew—and she was on board!"

"Uh...no, I didn't bring up the chair to Mom. You know how she feels about video games."

"Oh. Did you tell Goosy?"

"Nope."

Understandably, Dad looked puzzled. But I didn't know how to help him put his puzzle together without flushing Triple G down the toilet.

"Maybe they're getting me something secret just from them," I offered. It's amazing how you can be honest yet not <u>completely</u> tell the truth.

"Well, I guess it's natural to have a few secrets at Christmas time..."

"Yes. <u>Exactly!</u> In fact, it's probably best to keep it that way."

And, satisfied that Dad was giving the matter a rest, I got back to my homework. For geometry, I had to calculate the space inside a box, only the problem said it this way: "Compute the volume of this rectangular prism in cubic inches using the formula volume = length x width x height." I don't know why schoolbooks have to talk like Mr. Mot.

EASY PEESY. THE VOLUME OF THIS BOX IS 4 INCHES TIMES 3 INCHES TIMES 2 INCHES, WHICH EQUALS 24 CUBIC INCHES, WHICH EQUALS 24 SPOTS FOR A PERFECT CUBE OF FUDGE.

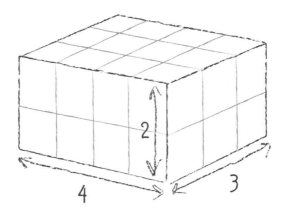

But as I was looking at the box I'd drawn for my homework, it started growing patterns and colors, right before my eyes. In my imagination, I mean. (What, do you think I'm going crazy just because I saw a stalker gnome in the mountains?!) The empty space started looking more like a container, and the top wall of the box started looking more like a lid. Then the patterns and colors formed into shapes, and pretty soon I was looking at a cool box that will be perfect for my mom's new ring! So I got out my art supplies and started making it for her.

She said she cherishes the things I hand-make. This ring box is gonna knock her Christmas-morning slippers off.

SO DOGGONE SAD

I helped Mr. Fodder in the school cafeteria after lunch today, like I have been all month. Since it was Pizza Monday, at least there wasn't much to clean up. I wheeled the salad bar back into the kitchen, which reminded me of the Classic Snow-Cone Cart, which made me think of only-8-more-days-till-Christmas!

"Hey, what are you gettin' for Christmas?" I asked him.

"It's pretty low-key at my house. Just me and Greta."

"She's your wife?"

"She's my Golden Retriever. How about you? Are you gonna get your hands on some good stuff?"

"Yeah. I think so!"

"Enjoy it while it lasts, kid."

Later, walking home with Jack, I gave some thought to what Mr. Fodder had said.

"My mom never wants <u>anything</u> for Christmas," added Jack.

"Mine either! When you get to be a certain age, does something happen to the part of your brain that recognizes awesomeness?"

"That would explain it."

"Sheesh. At least I'm making the most of this Christmas, while I still can. And I know you downsized your list, but don't worry...you can have unlimited snow-cone refills at my house whenever you want. Gratis.*"

I'm generous* like that.

I LOVE PI!

I thought I'd mastered shapes in preschool. But this geometry unit has me realizing there's way more to them than meets the eye.

Mr. Krug taught us about circles today in math. Did you know that the exact center of a circle is named the *origin*? I didn't either. And if you draw a straight line from the origin to the edge of the circle, it's called the *radius*. But here's the coolest thing of all: there's a number called *pi* that's like a magic formula just for circles. It's 3.14, and in numbers language you write it like this: π.

Using pi, you can measure the distance around a circle (because a ruler doesn't do curves). If you take 2 times the radius then multiply that number times pi, *bam!* You've got the circle's circumference (which, if the circle is in the form of a ball, is basically its belt size).

Huh. Grown-ups sometimes say "your circle" when they're talking about your friends and your family people. I guess that means I'm the origin of my circle! I think I've always suspected that.

Starting at me/the origin, here's how I'd draw out my Triple G plan:

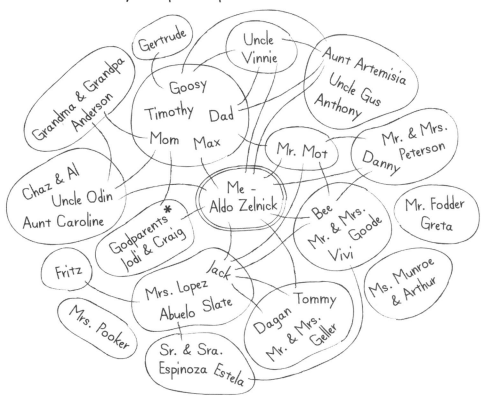

Other than Mom, Dad, and Goosy (oh, and Uncle Vinnie, since he texted Dad a clue, and Aunt Caroline, because she asked Mom about the all-terrain scooter), I don't remember who I asked for what. But I'm learning that when you harness the power of pi, like I did with Triple G, you're setting something powerful in motion. Just 7 more days till I find out what.

DEAR SANTA 2

I just got home from mailing a follow-up note to the head elf himself. Don't judge me. I'm fully aware that 10 is on the top rung of the ladder to the North Pole.. but sometimes when you're feeling unsure about things and you can't ask your parents, you've gotta go over their heads to a higher authority, right?

IT'D BE SO MUCH EASIER IF HE JUST GAVE OUT HIS EMAIL ADDRESS!

Before I mailed the letter, I snuck Griswold into my fort closet and

MR. CLAUS
NORTH POLE

ALDO ZELNICK
(YOU KNOW THE PLACE)
FORT COLLINS, CO

EMAIL IS FOR SISSIES.

read it to him out loud, just to be sure he was getting the message too. Here's what it said:

December 19

Dear S.C.,

Since you keep track, you probably know this is my second letter this year. I'm not trying to <u>replace</u> my first letter, though. All the stuff I put in that one is still on the table. But I do have a few things to <u>add</u>.

They're not things for me though! It's just, I found myself looking at my circle again today and realizing that some of the people in it might want presents they don't have the gumption* to ask for. Take Jack, for example. The guy's in love with rocks. He'll probably marry them if he can. If you just grabbed one for him from every country you visit, he'd be ecstatic. And Bee...I don't know if you give out livestock, but if you do, hook her up with a goat, wouldja? Mr. Mot always needs more books, and Goosy is all about artsy-fartsy stuff. My mom and dad could use a new car because our minivan is as old as me.

$\longrightarrow$

(CONTINUED FROM PAGE 1)

I bet Tommy Geller would go crazy for Dungeons & Dragons gear, but please go ahead and wrap his present in blue and write Happy Holidays on the tag. All my other circle people have been nice too, as far as I know, and deserve something good.

Ask and you'll get. That's what I learned in Sunday school. So I'm asking—on behalf of all the people who aren't brazen enough to ask for themselves. (Because being brazen is one gift I seem to have received in more than my fair share.)

See you in 6! Your fan,

Aldo Zelnick

1 IS THE
LONELIEST NUMBER

Gah! I couldn't sleep last night because of this circle business. Now it has me worried about more of my people! I mean, what if some of them don't get <u>any</u> presents! Wouldn't that be the worst...to wake up on Christmas morning and have nothing but your eyelids to open?

So after school today, I called up Goosy and Jack and Bee, and asked them if they'd help me with Project GASP—Give Awesomeness to Single People.

"Love it!" Goosy said. She drove to my house right away with gobs of art supplies. I carried Griswold over to the project table, so he could see up close how nice I was being. Then when Bee and Jack arrived a few minutes later, we got to work.

"OK, first up is Great-Aunt Gertrude. She lives in Georgia, and she's like 95," I said. "Wait... let me make sure she's not dead." I ran to ask Mom, who confirmed she's not, so I made her a picture frame out of popsicle sticks covered in glitter. I put a picture of my face inside it.

Meanwhile, Goosy and Jack discussed whether or not to make something for Mr. Mot. "He'll probably get presents from someone," I agreed, "but I don't think we should take any chances."

"I'd bet my gluteus maximus* he'd like a bookmark," suggested Goosy. And they made him a fancy leather bookmark with his name stamped into it.

Next: Mr. Fodder. "I could make him another framed picture of me," I suggested to the group.

"Nah," said Jack. "He sees your face too much already. But he is a foodie. Do you have any extra Christmas cookies we could give him?"

"We've got something even better: fudge. Dad and I made a batch of peanut-butter-chocolate-swirl just last night. I'll box him up some!"

Then, while I kept working on gewgaws* for the other GASPers in my circle, Bee and Jack made things for theirs. By the end of the night, we each had a nice little giving pile. Goosy helped us wrap everything and tie on tags that said, "Don't open till Christmas!" She also packaged up the presents that have to be mailed. She's gonna take them to the post office tomorrow morning.

Man, thinking of other people is hard work. I'm so tired that sleep sounds better than a before-bed snack. I don't think that's ever happened before.

THIS FRIDAY NIGHT

Woo-hoo! Christmas vacation has officially started! Two weeks of feasting and presents and NO SCHOOL.

Let us now bow our heads for a silent moment of thanks.

> WHEN YOU'RE DIGITAL, EVERY MOMENT IS SILENT.

After our final geometry test this afternoon (which I totally crushed), we had a Christmas holiday party in Mr. Krug's class. The mom squad laid out a cookie spread, and we got to play Holiday Charades instead of doing science and history. I stumped everyone when I acted out putting on a bowl-cap and lighting a menorah.

"I'm not sure which is better—the moment you get out of school at Christmas break or the same moment for summer vacation," I said to Jack as we were walking home.

"The thing about Christmas break is that it's a big long party for <u>everyone</u>," said Jack. "Summer vacation is just for kids."

"Hm. Not everyone celebrates Christmas, though... But, I guess it's 2 weeks' vacation either way," I said.

When I got home, nobody else was here, so I cranked up the song "Grandma Got Run Over By A Reindeer" really loud on the family-room iPod speakers. Griswold and Max and I did a little celebration dance. And now it's time to head out for dinner at Bee's family's restaurant! G2G.*

The Goodes opened a restaurant called Fare last month. But it's not just fair—it's great! During the meal, I sat by Bee. Her dad was busy helping in the kitchen, but her mom and sister sat with us.

YOU'RE NOT STILL GOING WITH THAT GREEDY MCSNEEDY PLAN OF YOURS, ARE YOU?

IT'S CALLED TRIPLE G. AND IT'S 4 SHORT DAYS FROM RAINING GIFTS UPON ME.

"But I thought you realized you needed to focus more on giving than getting," Bee said.

"Funny you should say that." I chewed on a chip smothered in guacamole.* "With your help, I did reconsider. So since then, as you've seen with your own 2 eyes, I've been handmaking lots of gifts. And I've been taking steps to be sure that the people in my circle get more presents."

"But you still have outrageous requests in to all your relatives?"

"Well, 'outrageous' is a pretty strong word..."

"And you've still got it fixed so that your mom and dad and Goosy are each getting you an expensive gift that the others don't know about?"

"Can I help it they love me so much?"

"You're exasperating!" she shouted. Frankly, I don't know how such loudness can come out of such a small person.

I slunk underneath the table and pulled her down there with me.

"Shhh! All right, how about if I share with you," I whispered.

"What?"

"Yeah, I'll let you borrow my Backyard Inflatable Log Flume for 1 week every summer, holidays and really hot days excluded."

"3 weeks. And 2 of those weeks we set it up in the park so all the neighborhood kids can use it."

"Great idea! How much you think we can charge per ride? A quarter?"

"For free! They get to use it for free! It's called sharing. You may have heard of it before."

"Oh all right."

"And after dinner, when I suggest that we all go caroling, you're going to enthusiastically agree."

"Gah! That's blackmail!"

"That's the game of life, pal."

And then, when I climbed back onto my chair, guess who was sitting in it? Griswold! In shock, I picked him up and looked around.

Mom noticed. "You brought Griz to dinner! That's so sweet!"

"But..."

"Tryin' to butter him up?" asked Timothy.

"I didn't... Someone must've..."

"That's such a good idea, Aldo!" cried Bee in her loud voice. "I bet Griswold would <u>love</u> to go caroling!"

So caroling we went, door-to-door. It's like trick-or-treating except you sing instead of get candy. Naturally, my "12 Days of Christmas: the Hungry Version" got big applause. In between houses, I asked around, trying to figure out who was the prankster who brought Griswold along. It wasn't me. <u>I</u> put him back on the fireplace mantel after our "Grandma Got Run Over By A Reindeer" celebration dance. And everyone else denied doing it. So ???????????????????

THE GIVING TREE

"You and Timothy need to go to with me to the mall today," Mom said this afternoon. She was sitting at the dining room table—the one that should be called the "whatever table" because we use it for whatever needs doing except for eating—amongst a mountain of wrapping paper and ribbon.

"Gadzooks, you're right!" I remembered. "Those Cinnabons aren't gonna eat themselves. Well, if they did, that would be super weird..."

"Not to snack, Aldo...to deliver the Giving Tree gifts. I just finished wrapping them. And we need to get going, because today's the last day to drop them off."

"Dang. I never got a chance to put Gimli* together."

"What?"

"Never mind."

When we got there, I noticed that the mall shoppers seemed more frantic than festive. They should have done their holiday shopping early, like I did.

We finally squeezed our way through to the Giving Tree, and my mouth fell open. Even with Triple G, I didn't have the gall* to imagine that many presents. The tree looked like it was planted on a tiny island surrounded by an <u>ocean</u> of presents. If I ever got deserted on an island like that, all those presents could keep me happy for centuries.

"Whewww...," Timothy whistled. "How many kids' names were hanging on that tree, anyway?"

"Amazing, isn't it," said Mom.

"It's heart-stopping," I said. It was true—seeing all of those presents and knowing not even one of them was for me kinda squeezed my heart in a funny way.

At the ocean's edge, I set down the box and gift bags for Griffin I was carrying. Timothy, of course, had to make it more challenging. He carried the presents for his kid across the ocean, leaping from one tiny bare spot of ground to another, until he got them right up under the tree.

While Timothy was busy jumping, Mom ran into Mrs. Goode, and the two of them started gibber-gabbering. I took the opportunity to pull something from my pocket and slip it into Griffin's gift bag. It was a Christmas tree ornament I'd made for him during Project GASP, even though kids usually aren't Single People (that *Home Alone* kid being the legendary exception).

When I looked up, I though I saw, out of the corner of my face, a triangle hat and googly eyes pop up from the gift ocean. But when I turned my head to get a better look, nothing was there except presents as far as my eyes could see.

Go ahead and spy on me, gnome dome. I don't care. I've got nothing to hide.

To Griffin, From Aldo.
MERRY CHRISTMAS
OR
HAPPY HOLIDAYS
(CIRCLE THE ONE YOU'RE MOST COMFORTABLE WITH.)

GUILTY?

GAH! HE'S EVERYWHERE! → 23

Oh geez, I think I did away with Griswold.

I'm in my bed. It's still dark outside and I'm groggy, but I have a very clear memory of Griz taunting me, telling me he was going to reveal all the details of Triple G to Santa AND my parents. He was giddy* with power. He tipped his little pink nose skyward and howled, "Mine! You're finally mine, Zelnick!"

So I'm NOT A GOODY TWO-SHOES!* NO KID IS! WELL, MAYBE BEE...

So...I snapped. I tossed him into the driveway and drove over him with my bike. I jumped off my bed and clotheslined him turnbuckle-style. I even, I think, poked him with my mom's gift-wrapping scissors. Everybody knows that Gnomes in the Home are made of indestructible foam, so I recall that I was having a hard time making a dent. But he <u>has</u> to be a goner* after all that, doesn't he?

I've gone nutty as a Christmas fruitcake! The minimum sentence for gnomicide* has to be a lifetime of no presents...without parole. Gah! A giftless existence! And I'm only 10!

I'm gonna go see if I can find his broken little body and glue him back together.

Oh happy day! I raced downstairs, and there was Griswold all in one piece, chillaxing on the fireplace mantel, just like always. I must've had a bad dream, that's all!

"Hey! You look totally fine!" I said, relieved as all get-out.*

He looked at me.

"What? OK, how 'bout this: I won't charge the other kids $2 for snow cones. I'll only charge a buck."

He looked at me   some more.

"Oh all right. <u>Free</u>. And how about this: Later today I'll borrow money from my next allowance to buy Jack that goethite geode he wants. There. Are you happy? I give and I give..."

OF GRUNTWORK*
AND GRACE

All this thinking-about-other-people gobbledygook* sure has its drawbacks.

Christmas Eve day is <u>supposed</u> to be filled up by a leisurely video-game session with Jack. But when I woke up this morning and shuffled past the bathroom mirror, I noticed my squigglier-than-usual hair, which made me think of bowl-hats and how they slide off my head so it's a good thing I didn't inherit Jewishness from my great-grandfather. (But the real deal-breaker, which I just found out

yesterday from Dad, is that Jews don't eat bacon!
What?!) Which made me remember that I never got
a Christmas present for Tommy Geller. Gah!

So I got Dad to take me to the store, where
I picked out a gyroscope* for Tommy, and I grabbed
Timothy golf tees because I'm nice, and I noticed
a pair of lady socks with birds on them,
so I put those in the cart for Mom.

"What about Bee?" Dad asked.

"I can't give a girl a Christmas present!" The
5th grade line between having a friend who's a girl
and having a girlfriend is skinnier than Jack's ankles.

Dad peered over the top of his glasses at
me. That's the grown-up look that means, *Fact-
check that statement with your conscience.*
And your conscience is basically the Gnome
in Your Gut.

So I sighed and went back for the lady socks
with bees on them I'd also noticed. Then as
we were checking out I remembered I still
needed to go to the rock store for Jack's geode,
so we stopped there on the way home.

Then I had to wrap all the stuff that I
borrowed future allowances to buy, and I had
to walk to Jack's and Tommy's and Bee's to
bring them their presents in case I don't see them
tomorrow. Between all that and the snow-
shoveling and tidying and kitchen-helper chores
Mom and Dad gave me and Timothy
this afternoon (and me making sure
Griswold saw or at least heard
about every good deed), the day
disappeared like that.   ⟶

SNAP

Goosy and Mr. Mot came for dinner, then all
6 of us went to night church. It's always packed
on Christmas Eve, so we got there early to get
a good pew. (A good pew...hahaha.) We listened
to the baby Jesus story, about him being born in a
barn and the angels scaring the bejeebers out of the
shepherds, and we watched the handbell choir, and
I was just getting uber warm and sleepy when it
was time to stand up in the dark church, hold up
our lit candles, and sing "Silent Night."

Afterwards, as we tramped to our car, we saw my friend Danny and his family in the parking lot, so we went over to talk to them. Danny's deaf, so he talks with his hands. He was gesticulating* like crazy, but I didn't understand, and the grown-ups who could interpret were busy with their own conversation, so he grabbed me by my arm, yanked me over to the church lawn, and shoved me backward into the snow. Then before I could yell for help, he plopped down next to me and started swinging his arms and legs.

Snow angels! While snowflakes swirled down at us from the toasted marshmallow sky, Danny and I made gossamer* snow angels all over the church lawn.

When I got home I put out pickles and chocolate milk for Santa, because...you never know.

And now...yawn...I'm so beat from all today's activities that I think I'm actually gonna be able to fall asleep! On Christmas Eve I usually try to stay awake as long as I can, hoping for a glimpse of the Gluttonous* Giver, the Big Elf Himself. But tonight, all I want to do is close this sketchbook, crash back onto my pillow (covered in the red flannel reindeer pillowcase my mom always slips onto it on Christmas Eve—nice touch, Mom), and not open my eyes till morning. <u>Christmas</u> morning. And what a <u>glorious</u> Christmas morning it's going to be.

GHERKINS AND CHOCOLATE MILK ALL SET FOR SANTA. HEY, A PROMISE IS A PROMISE!

CHRISTMAS  DAY

I woke up first and crept downstairs. It was just getting light out, but the Christmas tree lights were on, so without flipping a switch I could see that under...well, next to...the tree sat THE HUGEST PRESENT I HAVE EVER SEEN.

It was way taller than me and wider than a refrigerator. Could it be the Classic Snow-Cone Cart, I wondered? Or is it an iPhone, packed inside a box packed inside a box packed inside a box, like Timothy's was for his birthday? Or could it be not 1 but 2 video-game chairs, so Jack won't have to sit on the floor while I play?

I turned to Griswold. The Christmas stockings at his feet now bulged with gifts.

"What's in the big box, Griz?"

"You've been a good kid," he squeaked. "It's the All-Terrain Electric Transporter."

Just kidding. He kept his secrets, like he always does.

Around the bottom of the uber-gift sat a usualish amount of presents, some with my name, some with Timothy's, a few that said Mom or Dad or Goosy.

I turned around to go wake up my parents and Timothy, but there they stood, in the opening to the family room. Goosy too!

I jumped. "Geez! You guys scared the Grapenuts out of me!"

"We want to watch you open your big present, Aldo," said Mom. "Merry Christmas." And she gave me a smothery mom hug.

"But the big present is for last," I reminded them.

"Not this year, sport," said Dad.

"If you insist!" Everyone gathered round while I stood on a stepladder and tore off the shiny paper. Underneath was a plain cardboard box with a bunch of little holes poked into it. Weird. And the cardboard smelled kinda weird, like barns and flower gardens mixed together.

All of a sudden came a muffled achoo. "Gesundheit!*" I said automatically. "Hey! Who sneezed?

"Time to open the box!" cried Goosy.

"Quit movin' like a glacier,* bro!" said Timothy.

So I popped open the top of the box, but before I could peer down inside, the front of the box fell open all by itself and...

"Ahhh!" I screamed. "There are people in this box!"

"They're <u>your</u> people, my little gold digger,*" cried Goosy. "Instead of sending you extravagant gifts, they flew in to spend the holiday with you! Except Mr. Fodder. He was just walking by with Greta about an hour ago, so we invited them in."

It took a while for the crushing hugs and the "gotcha*" noogies and the loud gibber-gabber to dissipate. But after that, Dad broke out the Christmas morning cinnamon rolls and the egg casserole—both done up in triple batches, so it quieted down considerably when the feeding began.

"Aldo, did you really think we'd get you a $2,500 scooter?" teased Aunt Caroline.

Everybody laughed.

"Seemed like a good idea at the time," I mumbled.

"The kid asked me for a geodesic dome!*" croaked Great-Aunt Gertrude.

"Oh yeah! I forgot about that!" I said. "And later on, after I put it on my list, I learned about them in geometry! I still <u>do</u> want a geodesic dome!"

The crowd guffawed* some more. They were all in such good moods that they sucked me into one too.

Since we all of a sudden had so many guests, we didn't even open anymore Christmas presents today! Except for the sleds. My parents gave all the kids new sleds, so Timothy and I went sledding with our cousins Chaz and Al, then after cookies and hot chocolate, I called up my friends and we all built a snow menagerie in the field by my house. Jack and Tommy made a snow grizzly bear. Uncle Vinnie put together a groundhog, because he says a famous one lives close to him in Pennsylvania. Chaz and Al (they're twins) snow-sculpted a 2-headed gila monster.* Goosy and Mr. Mot did a gnu,* and my mom made a golden eagle to sit on top of it. Aunt Caroline and Uncle Odin rolled a cool giant panda. Timothy and Tommy built a gazelle. Using Greta as a model, Mr. Fodder packed together a Golden Snowtriever. Because I was wondering about my Giving Tree person today, I made a Griffin.* And Bee made...can you guess? Yup. A goat.

THERE'S NO BUSINESS LIKE SNOW BUSINESS.

It was a good day, but it was <u>not</u> Triple G. Welp, at least I still have presents to open tomorrow.

DECEMBER 28

After breakfast and seeing off Aunt Caroline, Uncle Odin, and the twins this morning for their drive back to Minnesota, I went with Goosy to take Great-Aunt Gertrude and Uncle Vinnie to the airport. When we got there, Goosy showed us where they'd installed her glass tree sculpture. And guess what? She hadn't made glass presents to put under it after all.. She'd made more glass trees to go around it!

"After you said it looked lonely, Aldo, I realized that what a tree needs isn't gifts. It needs other trees!"

She was right. When you stood back and looked at it from a distance, a glass <u>forest</u> seemed more...gratifying.*

When I hugged Great-Aunt Gertrude and Uncle Vinnie, Uncle Vinnie told me to never stop being a go-getter.* I think that means it's OK for me to keep asking him for presents.

And now...I guess this is the part where I have to admit what I got for Christmas.

When we finally opened presents the next day, I got almost everything that was on the piece of my list I'd given to Mom: socks, pajamas, and legos—plus a couple of books, one video game, and a little glass Grinch ornament, from Goosy.

Mom <u>loved</u> the ring box I made, which was cool, and Dad did a little cheese dance of love over his new grater.

Still, I was feeling kinda glum* when Dad reminded me that we hadn't unstuffed our stockings yet. I dashed over to grab mine then dropped to the floor and dumped it out onto the rug.

Besides a nice bunch of candy, my stocking stash included a lump of coal (true), 3 pairs of Green Lantern underwear, and...a blue cell phone. It's not an iPhone, but at least it's <u>my</u> phone.

The first person I called was Jack, and the second person was Bee, and then Danny and Tommy. I gave them all my new phone number, and I invited them to come over for a fort party on New Year's Eve. Dad said he'd make us homemade pizza and ice cream. That's way better than dumb snow cones anyway, doncha think?

"G" GALLERY

Mr. Mot used to be an English teacher. He's a word nerd, and he likes to help me use awesome words in my sketchbooks. I mark the best words with one of these: * (it's called an asterisk). When you see an * you'll know you can look here, in the Gallery, to see what the word means. If you don't know how to say some of the words, just ask Mr. Mot. Or someone you know who's like Mr. Mot. Or go to aldozelnick.com, and we'll say them for you.

G (pg. 7): cool guy

gabbed (pg. 87): talked a bunch

gadgets (pg. 17): little things that do helpful stuff

gadzooks! (pg. 50): holy smokes! wow!

I'M GAGA FOR GUMMI WORMS

gaga (pg. 56): crazy

galore (pg. 29): gobs of

gall (pg. 123): guts of braveness

gaffes (pg. 64): mistakes

gallery (pg. 10 and this page): a place where you group awesome things

gallivanting (pg. 94): going all over the place

galumph (pg. 89): walk with clumsiness

gangly (pg. 87): long, skinny, and awkward

gaping (pg. 44): staring and staring

garbanzo (pg. 17): a round, white bean you smush up to make a dip called hummus. Tastes better than it sounds.

gargantuan (pg. 79): super-huge; way bigger than you'd expect

garnet (pg. 56): a dark red gemstone that Jack says is semi-precious, and that means it costs just a semi-a lot of money

garnish (pg. 86): a finishing touch, just for looks

PARSLEY IS PERFECT!

gaseousness (pg. 52): a fancier way of saying gassy-ness, which you know what that means

gasped (pg. 56): making a noise when you suck air in. It means you're surprised.

gaudy (pg. 47): decorated too much, so that it's gone past looking good and has rounded the corner into looking junky

gawking (pg. 35): pretty much staring at, even less politely than gaping

gaze (pg. 32): look at steady, but with your eyes not quite so wide open as gawking

145

gazillion (pg. 82): a really lot, like a million million or something

gefilte fish (pg. 63): cold fish meatloaf. Tastes...weird.

gender stereotypes (pg. 79): what people think boys should do or girls should do (but really, either can do anything)

generous (pg. 103): good at sharing without expecting something back

genius (pg. 31): see "Zelnick, Aldo" in the Z sketchbook someday

geodesic dome (pg.139): a building shaped like a sphere, but the sphere is actually made up of little triangles

geometry (pg. 40): math that you can draw because it's about shapes and angles

gerbil (pg. 8, 11): like a mouse except larger and with smaller ears, bigger eyes, and a furry tail

gesticulating (pg. 132): moving your hands while you talk

Gesundheit (pg. 137): German way to say "good health" when someone sneezes

get a glimmer (pg. 59): have a little bit of under-standing about

THERE'S NO PLACE LIKE MY GERBIL DOME HOME!

get a grip (pg. 83): This means: You're talking like you're better than everyone else, but you're not.

get my goat (pg. 67): make me mad; trip my trigger; push my buttons

get-out, as all (pg. 128): expression that means the maximum amount

gewgaws (pg. 114): unnecessary decorations; bric-a-brac

geyser (pg. 50): like a volcano that shoots water and steam instead of lava

gherkin (pg. 7, 66): a tiny pickle

OLD FAITHFUL
NEXT ERUPTION IN 40-100 MIN

(NOT GINORMOUS.)

gibber-gabbered (pg. 90): chatted in a way that boy kids get bored with. Can also be spelled jibber-jabbered.

giddy (pg. 126): so happy that you're kind of silly with happiness

gifted (pg. 43): something good you're just born with

gila monster (pg. 140): a real lizard whose poisonous bite can kill you

Gimli (pg. 122): that funny, curmudgeonly dwarf in Lord of the Rings

ginormous (pg. 61): so big you gasp

gizmos (pg. 12): gadgets*

glacier (pg. 137): a giant ice cube in the North or South Pole oceans (and sometimes on land, like in the high mountains) that's so big it never melts

glimpsed (pg. 93): a tiny look at

glitch (pg. 34): a little problem that is just annoying. This happens a lot in video games.

gloating (pg. 89): bragging

glorious (pg. 29): so wonderful it's heavenly

gloom (pg. 31): darkness

glowered (pg. 90): frowned

glum (pg. 142): sad

gluteus maximus (pg. 113): scientific term for butt

gluttonous (pg. 134): eats way too much

gnome (pg. 35): a magical creature with a pointy head that's somewhere between an elf and a fairy and a dwarf

gnomicide (pg. 127): um..."icide" means killing something, so...

gnu (pg. 140): an African animal that looks halfway between an antelope and an ox; pronounced "new"

go-getter (pg. 142): somebody who has gumption*

gobbledygook (pg. 129): nonsense

GNOMES ARE REAL?! I "GNU" IT!

gobs (pg. 19): lots of

godparents (pg. 108): the grown-ups your parents pick to take care of you if anything ever happens to them

goethite geode (pg. 26): a kind of rusty rock with a surprise center

gold-digger (pg. 138): somebody who's just after getting lots of expensive stuff or money

goner (pg. 127): dead

goody two-shoes (pg. 126): somebody who always does what's right. I think I'm a goody one-shoe.

goofy (pg. 85): silly and weird mixed together

goon (pg. 92): a dumb, awkward person

gorgeous (pg. 12): really nice-looking

Gorgon (pg. 32): a mythological creature with snakes for hair that turns you to stone just by looking at you

gormless (pg. 37): dumb

gory (pg. 21): messy and gross

gossamer (pg. 132): delicate and wispy

gossip (pg. 8, 92): talking about somebody when they're not there

gotcha (pg. 139): caught doing something you maybe weren't supposed to be doing

Grand Canyon (pg. 16): a great big canyon somewhere below Colorado

grandeur, delusions of (pg. 59): when you think you're more important than you actually are

granola (pg. 15): a cereal mixture with little pieces of grains and nuts and fruit that's supposed to be good for you

gratifying (pg. 142): giving you a feeling of happy rightness

gratis (pg. 103): free

greedy (pg. 14): wanting more than your fair share

Greek yogurt (pg. 15): yogurt that's thicker than usual

griffin (pg. 140): a mythical creature with the body of a lion and the head and wings of an eagle; also a boy's name

gridlock (pg. 55): so many people you can barely move

grimaced (pg. 88): made a funny face that means you're not happy

groggy (pg. 61): that dopey feeling you have when you just wake up

MMM, CRUNCHY.

groovy (pg. 14): cool and attractive

grotesque (pg. 97): icky-weird

groused (pg. 88): complained

grub (pg. 73): basic food

grueling (pg. 13): really hard and fatiguing, like gruntwork*

gruntwork (pg. 129): work that anybody can do but nobody wants to because it's tiring

G2G (pg. 116): got to go

guacamole (pg. 117): yummy green chip-dip; the reason avocados exist

guff (pg. 57): backtalk

guffawed (pg. 139): laughed loudly

guise (pg. 28): costume of; dressed up like

gullible (pg. 44): believing anything you're told

gulp (pg. 18): a swallowing sound

Gumby (pg. 17): this old-fashioned cartoon character guy who looks like a cross between a gingerbread man and a stick man

ACTUALLY, HE REMINDS ME OF BACON BOY...ONLY GREEN AND RUBBERY.

gumption (pg. 110): braveness mixed with wanting to accomplish something

gunk (pg. 85): gooey grossness

gussying up (pg. 95): making something look fancy

gyrating (pg. 92): turning and turning

gyros (pg. 17): yummy sandwiches made of a circle of soft pita bread folded in half and filled with lamb meat, lettuce, tomatoes, onions, and a white sauce that tastes like cucumbers

gyroscope (pg. 130): a complicated spinning toy made of 3 empty circles and a flat disc

MY NEIGHBORHOOD

To the North Pole

To wild tree hunting grounds (and sledding)

Bee's House

My House / Triple G HQ

Mr. Mot's House

Closed Pool

To Goosy's House

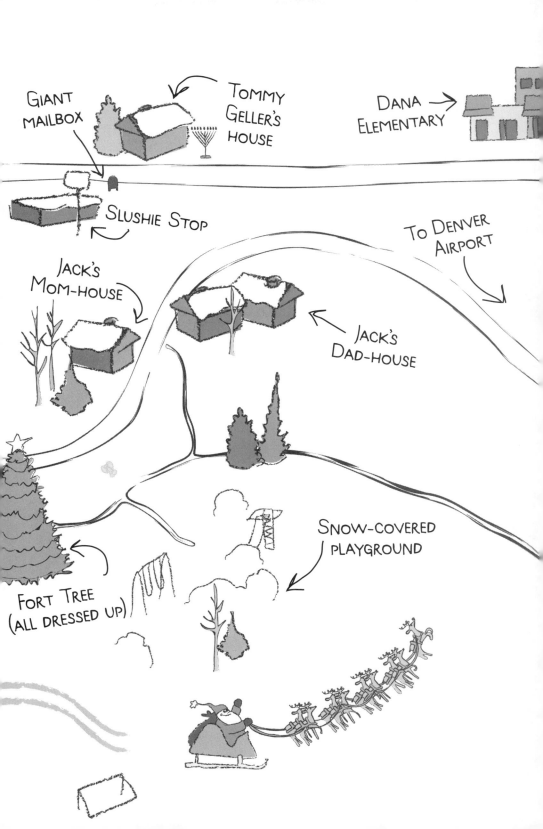

award-winning
v
ABOUT THE ALDO ZELNICK
COMIC NOVEL SERIES

The Aldo Zelnick comic novels are an alphabetical series for middle-grade readers aged 7-13. Rabid and reluctant readers alike enjoy the intelligent humor and drawings as well as the action-packed stories. They've been called vitamin-fortified *Wimpy Kids*.

NOW AVAILABLE!

160 pages | Hardcover
ISBN: 978-1-934649-04-6
$12.95

Part comic romps, part mysteries, and part sesquipedalian-fests (ask Mr. Mot), they're beloved by parents, teachers, and librarians as much as kids.

Artsy-Fartsy introduces ten-year-old Aldo, the star and narrator of the entire series, who lives with his family in Colorado. He's not athletic like his older brother, he's not a rock hound like his best friend, but he does like bacon. And when his artist grandmother, Goosy, gives him a sketchbook to "record all his artsy-fartsy ideas" during summer vacation, it turns out Aldo is a pretty good cartoonist.

In addition to an engaging cartoon story, each book in the series includes an illustrated glossary of fun and challenging words used throughout the book, such as *absurd, abominable*, and *audacious* in *Artsy-Fartsy* and *brazen, behemoth*, and *boisterous* in *Bogus*.

BAILIWICK PRESS

www.bailiwickpress.com | www.aldozelnick.com

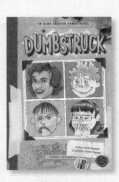

ACKNOWLEDGMENTS

*"We plunged into the cornucopia,
quivering with desire and the ecstasy
of unbridled avarice."*

— Ralphie, in *A Christmas Story*

Oh to be a kid at Christmas again.

Abundant goodies, sweet and savory. Decadent school-less days. Sledding, ice skating, and all manner of snow play. And glorious gifts galore! Detached from financial considerations, as they are to children, Christmas presents are essentially gift-wrapped glee. We hope you won't judge our young Greedy McSneedy too harshly. After all, he's just starting to learn that Christmas doesn't come from a store...that Christmas, perhaps, means a little bit more.

This coming-up-on-Christmas season we're genuinely grateful for Google (Truly! When you pack a gazillion references into books, as we do, you depend on it!); gal Monday through Friday Renée; the Slow Sanders, for guiding Aldo as he grows; Hanukkah mavens Ellen and Debby; and design guru Launie. And to our families and Aldo's Angels—thank you for both your generous love and your lovely generosity.

Merry Christmas! (And Happy Hanukkah!)

ALDO'S GREATHEARTED ANGELS

Halo There! If you're an Aldo Zelnick fan, e-mail info@bailiwickpress.com and ask for details about becoming an Aldo's Angel. Angels receive special opportunities such as pre-publication discounts, free shipping, naming rights, and listing in the acknowledgments (especially fun for kids).

Barbara Anderson

Carol & Wes Baker

Butch & Sue Byram

Annie Dahlquist

Michael & Pam Dobrowski

Leigh Waller Fitschen

Sawyer & Fielding Gray (and Chris & Sarah)

Roy Griffin

Calvin Halvorson & Bennett Zent (and Chet)

Oliver Harrison (and Matthew & Erin)

Terry & Theresa Harrison

Richard & Peggy Hohm

Chris Hutchinson

Anne & Calvin Keasling

Vicki & Bill Krug

Tutu, Papa, Cole, Grant & Iris Ludwin

Annette & Tom Lynch

Lisa & Kyle Miller

Kristin & Henry Mouton

The Motz & Scripps Families (McCale, Alaina, Caden & Ambria)

Jackie O'Hara & Erin Rogers

Betty Oceanak

Jackie Peterson

Ryan Petros

Terri & David Rosen

John Schiller & Suzanne Holm

Slow Sand Writers Society

Barb & Steve Spanjer

Dana Spanjer

Vince & Adrianne Tranchitella

Laura Welciek

THE ALDO ZELNICK FAN CLUB
IS FOR READERS OF ANY AGE WHO
LOVE THE BOOK SERIES AND
WANT THE INSIDE SCOOP ON
ALL THINGS ZELNICKIAN.

GO TO WWW.ALDOZELNICK.COM
AND CLICK ON THIS FLAG-THINGY!

SIGN UP TO RECEIVE:

- sneak preview chapters from the next book.
- an early look at coming book titles, covers, and more.
- opportunities to vote on new character names and other stuff.
- discounts on the books and merchandise.
- a card from Aldo on your birthday (for kids)!

The Aldo Zelnick fan club is free and easy.
If you're under 13, ask your mom or dad to sign you up!

ABOUT THE AUTHOR

Karla Oceanak has been a voracious reader her whole life and a writer and editor for more than twenty years. She has also ghostwritten numerous self-help books. Karla loves doing school visits and speaking to groups about childhood literacy. She lives with her husband, Scott, and their three boys and a cat named Puck in a house strewn with Legos, ping-pong balls, Pokémon cards, video games, books, and dirty socks in Fort Collins, Colorado. This is her seventh novel.

ABOUT THE ILLUSTRATOR

Kendra Spanjer divides her time between being "a writer who illustrates" and "an illustrator who writes." She decided to cultivate her artistic side after discovering that the best part of chemistry class was entertaining her peers (and her professor) with "The Daily Chem Book" comic. Since then, her diverse body of work has appeared in a number of group and solo art shows, book covers, marketing materials, fundraising events, and public places. When she invents spare time for herself to fill, Kendra enjoys skiing, cycling, exploring, discovering new music, watching trains go by, decorating cakes with her sister, making faces in the mirror, and playing with her dog, Puck.